For Holly and William, with lots of love x
– Auntie Cally

For two little monkeys, Minna and Tom.
S.B.

First American Edition 2019
Kane Miller, A Division of EDC Publishing

Original English language edition first published in 2019 under the title *I Do it Like This!*
by Egmont UK Limited, The Yellow Building, 1 Nicholas Road, London, W11 4AN
Text copyright © Egmont UK Limited 2019
Illustrations copyright © Cally Johnson-Isaacs 2019
The Illustrator has asserted her moral rights.

For information contact:
Kane Miller, A Division of EDC Publishing
P.O. Box 470663
Tulsa, OK 74147-0663
www.kanemiller.com
www.edcpub.com
www.usbornebooksandmore.com

Library of Congress Control Number: 2018949199

Printed and bound in Malaysia
1 2 3 4 5 6 7 8 9 10
ISBN: 978-1-61067-826-1

I do it like this!

Written by Susie Brooks

Illustrated by Cally Johnson-Isaacs

Kane Miller
A DIVISION OF EDC PUBLISHING

All around the world, animals are making noises, moving around, eating, sleeping and playing. Some animals do things just like you . . . while others are very different!

How do you eat?

A chameleon SHOOTS out its tongue to catch food.

A chimpanzee SWINGS from tree to tree.

How do you move?

While you use words to chat to your friends,
a lion lets out a loud ROAR!

Let's find out how other animals do all these things –
as well as washing, keeping warm or cool, and lots more!

How do you eat?

Natalie eats like this,
with a bowl and a spoon to scoop up food.

Her teeth **munch** and **crunch**, then
GULP, she swallows!

A bird PECK PECKS with
its pointy beak. It doesn't
have any teeth!

A snake opens its mouth wide,
then SWALLOWS its food whole!

SLURP! A chameleon catches insects on its sticky, fast-flicking tongue.

When a panda is hungry, it picks plants with its GIANT paws.

Leaves are an easy snack for a snail, which has thousands of teeth on its tongue!

How do you move?

Tammy moves like this,
with a hop, **skip** and a **jump**!

BOING!
A kangaroo bounces.
Can you bounce too?

Tammy can walk very slowly
or run really fast.

Chimpanzees SWING through the trees, chitter-chattering!

A crab SCUTTLES sideways, instead of forward or back.

Who can paddle, waddle or fly? Quacking ducks!

How do you wash?

Jack washes like this
in a **warm bubbly bath**,
with soap and water to make him clean.

SPLASH!

An elephant SLURPS up water through its trunk.

Then it SQUIRTS the
water out like a shower!

A lion washes by
LICKING its fur.

WHEEE! Rolling in dust helps
a zebra SCRUB bugs off its back.

How do you tell things to your friends?

Lily chats on the telephone.
She can nod, wave, whisper,
shout or write messages too.

Male crickets rub their wings together to CHIRP to female crickets.

The bright colors of a poison dart frog WARN other animals not to eat it.

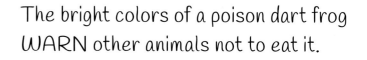

AWOOOOOOO!
Wolves call their pack together with a HOWL.

ROAR!

A lion's noisy ROAR can travel so far, it doesn't need a telephone!

How do you dance?

Jake dances like this, **leaping** and **twisting** and **waving** his arms . . .

He swivels in time to the music!

A male peacock spider HOPS and BOPS, shaking his legs and bottom in the air!

Honeybees dance in a FIGURE EIGHT to show each other where to find flowers.

How does a magnificent peacock boogie?
He shakes his TAIL FEATHERS
to impress peahens!

A giraffe's PATCHY MARKINGS
help it to hide safely among trees.

How do you hide?

Emma hides like this,
so no one can see her . . .

She keeps **very still** and tries
not to make a sound!

A pangolin curls up into
a ball when danger is near.

Is anybody there? Leaf geckos look like LEAVES, so hungry hunters can't spot them!

In snowy lands, a white polar bear blends in, to help it CREEP UP on its dinner.

How do you cuddle?

Dan cuddles like this, reaching out his arms and **squeezing tight.**

Orangutans cuddle just like we do. Their arms are very LONG and strong!

Parrots show love with a gentle NUZZLE. They stay with their loved ones for life.

Baby opossums have lots of brothers and sisters, who CLIMB all over their mom to give her a hug!

On a sunny day,
how do you keep cool?

Lucy keeps cool like this, sploshing and splashing in her wading pool.

The cape ground squirrel uses its tail as a SUNSHADE.

A dog keeps cool by sticking out its tongue and PANTING!

A hot hippo likes to WALLOW
in water or mud.

A shovel-snouted lizard does a little
DANCE, lifting two feet at a time so
the hot ground doesn't sizzle its toes!

 A bumblebee QUIVERS, a bit like we shiver, fluttering its wings to and fro.

A sheep grows its own woolly coat, thick and fluffy to keep out the cold.

When it's freezing outside, how do you keep warm?

Tess keeps warm like this, putting on a woolly hat and other cozy clothes.

The wool for Becky's hat came from a sheep!

In snowy weather, Japanese macaque monkeys love a BATH in a steaming hot spring.

How do chilly penguins warm up? They SNUGGLE together in a huddle!

How do you sleep?

Sarah sleeps like this in a comfy bed, curled up with her cuddly friends.

She shuts her eyes tight and dreams until morning.

A koala sleeps ALL DAY, and half the night too! When do you sleep?

Imagine FLYING while you sleep! A swift can!

Meerkats SNOOZE in heaps, deep in their burrows.

A dozy bat dangles UPSIDE DOWN . . .
and so does a sleepy sloth!

Sleeping sea otters HOLD PAWS so they
don't drift away from each other on the water.

We all do things in our own way,
but can you move and make noises
like these animals?

Ducks have webbed feet to help
them swim and paddle in water.

Can you waddle like a duck?

A chameleon's tongue is
twice as long as its body.

Stick out your tongue like a chameleon
– but try not to catch a fly!

Try scuttling sideways like a crab!

A crab's legs are attached to the
sides of its body and bend outward,
so it can only run left or right.

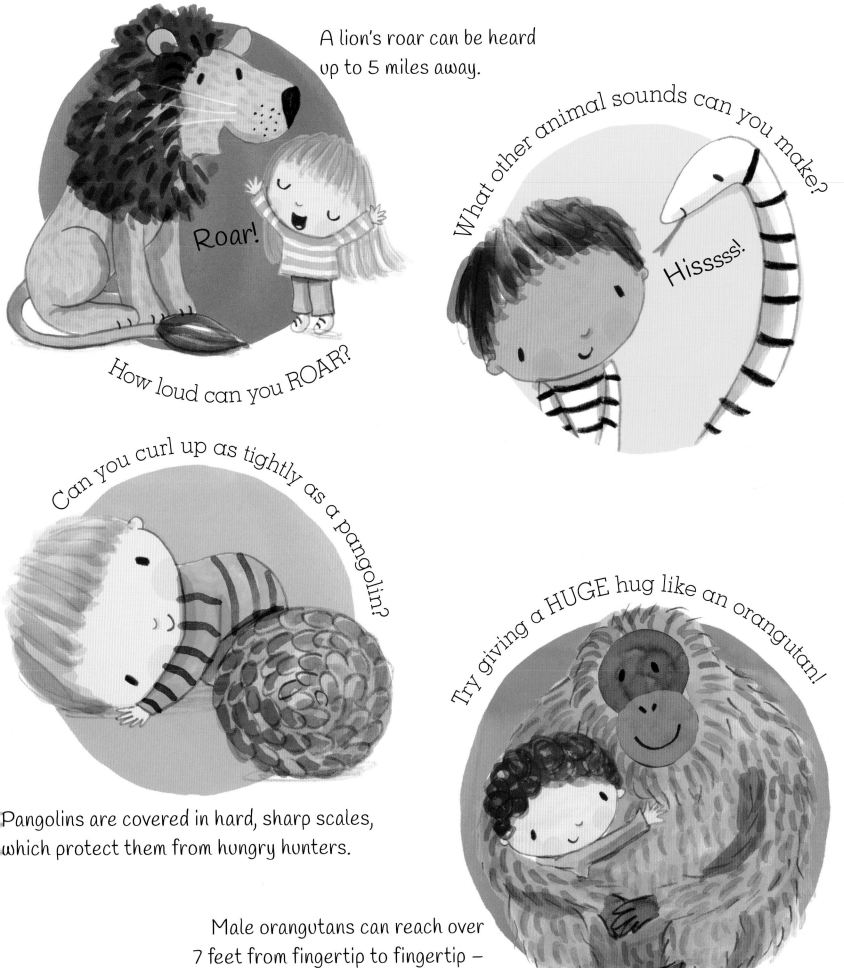

A lion's roar can be heard up to 5 miles away.

Roar!

How loud can you ROAR?

What other animal sounds can you make?

Hisssss!

Can you curl up as tightly as a pangolin?

Pangolins are covered in hard, sharp scales, which protect them from hungry hunters.

Try giving a HUGE hug like an orangutan!

Male orangutans can reach over 7 feet from fingertip to fingertip — that's longer than your bed!